WEIRDO SIMPATICO

Little Stories for Short Attention Spans

KATY BOURNE

Ray & Sharon,

Thank you to your enduring support & your willing to take a risk!

Katy

Dedicated to Henry Bourne.
There's so much of you in these stories.

TABLE OF CONTENTS

34 - 51

Quintessence

Propaganda

Dream

Undeterred

Universe

Success

Expression

Allowing

Narcissistic

Gay

Survived

Exciting

Swing

Silence

Gregarious

Harmony

Shenanigans

Imagine

ACKNOWLEDGMENTS

I'd like to thank Martha, Allen and Cindy Bourne for their love, enthusiasm and enduring support. Extra props to Martha for her willingness to be the human guinea pig for this project. I'd also like to send a big virtual high five to James Altucher. While many have inspired, James was the guy who kicked my butt into getting this done. And finally, I'd like to send big love out to everyone who contributed the words that inspired the book. These little stories are for you.

INTRODUCTION

A few years ago, I engaged in an interesting back and forth with friends on Facebook. I asked them to individually suggest single words, which I then used as springboards for crafting very short stories, which I posted on my page. At the time, I was counting down to the launch of my new website and this silly word game was a fun way to interact with potential fans and create a little buzz for the launch. The response was surprisingly enthusiastic. My friends liked watching me wrangle with the odd words they had thrown my way. I enjoyed the challenge of creating these tiny worlds for our collective entertainment.

Because we all had such a rollicking good time, I recently decided to have another go at it. I posted another request for words. My friends and fans humored me once again and offered up many interesting, cool and strange words for me to tackle. Instead of posting the stories on Facebook, I have compiled them here. This collection represents fifty of the words that were so graciously provided to me. The foibles, quirks and conundrums herein are mini snapshots that reflect our kooky humanity and the day-to-day challenges of living with each other. We are all weirdos here. And it's all good.

His was a power burp; a pinnacle of human achievement, a dazzling display of supreme bodily function. She hated him yet secretly admired him. But her dignity was on the line. She would have to double down. She would match his liter with two of her own. She grabbed the Pepsi and swilled voraciously, frantically. She would call the oceans home. She would shake the gods out of the sky. She would orchestrate chaos across the cosmos. She felt the rumble rising and grabbed the edge of the table with both hands. She would not let him win this. Not again. Not ever.

LOVE

Agnes wanted to be in love again, to feel the unmistakable tingle of loin and bosom. Every inch of Walter delighted her, from the hairs in his nose to his weathered work boots. The time was now. She inched closer. Barely breathing, she grabbed his calloused hand. High above, the planets and the stars smiled. Today, they would give her a win.

"There is a direct linkage between eating glue and brain tumors," their mother chided, "And studies show that children who throw dirt are more likely to become career criminals." Cosmo and Dexter nodded quietly and kicked at each other under the table. They were unashamed but knew better than to argue. All they wanted was for her to stop talking and pour the chocolate milk.

PENUMBRA

He wanted to be her supernova. He wanted to blaze through her heart and wreak the kind of havoc that only the best of lovers can do. He wanted to eclipse the day itself and disorient her completely. He stayed up late at night, dizzy at the possibility. Yet in the cruel snap of morning, he watched her laugh and carry on with the other fellows. Deep down he knew that he was, at best, merely a sigh or a glance; a lonesome penumbra on a long forgotten moonscape.

Zelda pulled on her boots and grabbed her pistol. She was done with the drunken frat boys and their pickup trucks. She was fed up with their pissing on her tomato plants. She was tired of being referred to as "the dumb hick with the bad teeth." She stood on the porch, took aim and let the education begin.

ANTIDISESTABLISHMENTARIANISM

"Antidisestablishmentarianism."

Roxanne wrinkled her nose. "This again," she thought as she looked at the panel. She glanced at the moderator. He looked so dreary in his Dockers and his comb over. She stepped up to the microphone, effortlessly spelled the word and quietly dreamed of a day when her parents did not need for her to be a champion.

Darrell had reason for his optimism. His truck was running real good. Home Depot gave him a raise. He'd almost paid off the flat screen. He watched the fine ladies walk across the Safeway parking lot. They were so checking him out. He gave them a sexy nod and a quick grin. Every damn thing was falling into place. He could feel it. He spit into the Styrofoam cup, leaned against his truck and waited.

CALM

His heart was rumbling like a monster truck but Walter remained calm. Her hand was soft and delicate. She smelled of Ivory soap and lemon drops. Bewildered but determined, he returned her timid squeeze. All of the sudden, none of it—the broken down forklift, the late delivery, the inebriated foreman—mattered. He knew that in this instant, everything was changing forever.

Dee Dee was empowered by her hot pink Grecian swimsuit and her flamingo swim cap. She stood on the end of the diving board and adjusted her goggles. The rude little children laughed and pointed. "Pshaw to them," she breezed as she made her enormous leap, drenching them all in her brilliance.

VICTORY

They were sweaty and exhausted, but the victory was hers. The shattered glass from the windows proved it, as did the cracks in the drywall. A few dozen Pepsi bottles were scattered around the kitchen floor. He rubbed his head, still stunned by her raw prowess and complete mastery. He knew he had work to do. But this was not over.

Debbie knew that despite his "Namaste" this and "Namaste" that, Doug was actually an asshole. He yelled at the dog, left his socks and underwear strewn around the house and never helped with the dishes. She watched him smiling and nodding at everyone. This picnic was a farce and these people were fools. She'd out the son-of-a-bitch someday. The world needed to know the truth.

RHINOPLASTY

Eugene was resolute. He would not pay for a third rhinoplasty. "You already look like a duck," he reasoned, "This freak show is breaking the bank." But his wife begged and cajoled. She only wanted a few finishing touches. Tired of her endless haranguing, Eugene considered his options. He watched videos on You Tube and researched over-the-counter anesthetics. "How hard could this be?" he thought to himself, "It's not like it's brain surgery."

TRUST

Gloria did not trust the neighbor's dog. He looked like Ernest Borgnine and he slobbered. A lot. She did not care for his furtive glances or the way that he grunted when she walked up the gravel driveway. She long suspected that it was not she he was interested in but the contents of her grocery bag. The dog was a phony baloney, up to no good.

HONESTY

"Honesty is overrated," Floyd said as he grabbed another doughnut off the tray. With coffee dribbling down the front of his shirt, he continued. "Nobody really cares how you feel or what your opinion is about this thing or that or the other. See, people don'ts got time for all that. They want short, quick and easy." He wiped his mouth on his sleeve. "They just wants you to shut up and git her done." His employees shifted in their seats, incredulous and crestfallen that fate had brought them to this place.

CACTUS

Hiding amongst the cactus was an ill-fated move, especially in her drunken state. But all hell had broken loose at the bachelorette party. The cops, the dogs and the cameras were too much for Elaine. Grabbing the last bottle of vodka on the way out the door, she ran into the dark desert and hoped for a positive outcome. The sting of the quills humbled her. Tomorrow or the next day, she would quit for good.

"Have you no moral compass?" the old woman said as she looked down her enormous nose at them. Cosmo and Dexter twitched and shuffled. She was the meanest librarian ever and she smelled like cough syrup. Cosmo abruptly threw the National Geographic at her head, and they ran shrieking for their lives.

LETTUCE

Blaire was a lettuce snob. He only wanted romaine and it had to be locally grown and organic. She wondered if she could live with such a relentlessly fussy man. She watched as he picked over the produce, scrutinizing every vegetable. She grabbed a head of iceberg and threw it in the cart. He looked up in disbelief. She straightened her shoulders. It was going to be a long night at the Safeway.

Baxter did not want to sleepwalk through life. He wanted to blow up this cubicle and shoot bottle rockets out of his nostrils. He was game to be a freak and to have people refer to him as otherworldly. He would give free rides to the moon and juggle the stars. And all the women of the world would fall in love with him. Every single one of them.

AZUCAR

He could not believe he was sitting at a bar next to Celia Cruz. How many shots had he had? Was there wine too? And wasn't she dead anyway? She smiled at him. "¡Azucar!" she cried with a raise of her glass. He took another nip of tequila, directly from the bottle this time. A feather from her very large headdress fell and tickled his nose. "¡Azucar!" she repeated. She filled the room with something he had never felt before. His confusion became irrelevant. He would go anywhere with this woman.

Every child was given a baked potato with a candle in it. The old man in the lawn chair muttered incoherently. And a donkey wandered around the back yard, nibbling on the bows of the packages. This was unlike any birthday celebration that Benny had ever been to. But being the new kid on the block, he had to accept every invitation, to seize any overture of kindness.

OKAY

"Somehow this is all going to be okay," Rufus thought to himself, "It will just take a little time. The forsythia will bloom again. The thick mountain snow will melt into ample creeks. The slow summer wind will tinkle through the chimes on the back porch. And she will change her mind. In spite of her stubborn heart, she will definitely change her mind."

Anna looked at the bejeweled backpack. Her grandmother was insane. There was no way she would take this to school. It was hideous and stupid and annoying. She did not understand old people. Everything about them was awkward and weird. Still, she gazed up from the package and smiled at her grandmother. "Thank you so much," she gushed, "You're the sweetest grandma on the planet, forever until the end of time."

DOG

The dog watched Gloria walk up the driveway and wondered what she had in the bag. He wandered closer and caught a whiff of beef. He contemplated his next move.

Gregoire took a quick spot check in the mirror. He straightened his ascot, smoothed a quick hand over his pompadour and popped a breath mint into his mouth. Tonight would be his. His pheromones were firing high. He would woo them with his excellentricity. The ladies would swoon over him. Oh yes, they would.

BOOM

Agnes ignored the first boom and then the second. After the third, she put her book down, got up from her chair, ambled to the front door and poked her head out. Debris was scattered all around the cul-de-sac. The air was putrid with the stench of smoke and sulfur. Cosmo and Dexter darted across the front lawn, screeching liked deranged banshees. Perhaps matches weren't such a good idea after all. Next time, she would give them colored pencils and sketch pads.

"Don't tell for me to take it to the chill pill," her grandfather barked in frustration. Roxanne rolled her eyes. "It's take a chill pill," she chirped back, "Not take it to the chill pill." She was tired of this conversation. She was tired of his head spinning around. She didn't care about her Eastern European lineage or her alleged bad manners. She was very clear; she would not friend her grandfather on Facebook.

SCHMOOZE

She was a kooky dingdong who could schmooze with the best of them. She had a six-inch beehive and generous breasts. Her bright red lips and nails were ferocious, and she moved through the room with a decisive lady swagger. She was a killer. He'd let her do all the talking.

Elaine fumbled through an oversized bag. Her enormous faux fur thrift shop overcoat smothered her tiny frame. There was a snag in her nylons, but her make-up was impeccable, albeit on the heavy side. "What? So I freak out sometimes," she snapped at her friend Brandy, "It's not like I'm a serial killer or a child molester." Brandy tightened her jaw. These conversations never went well. Elaine lit a cigarette. Brandy watched her blow smoke out of the side of her mouth and fiddle with her cell phone. "They just want someone to fuck with," she rambled, "And it's always me. Assholes." Brandy started to counter but stopped herself, opting instead just to listen. Love somehow found a way of always going the distance.

Percy did a flip, then another and another. He ran around the warm summer lawn, shouting in Pig Latin. He had no clue where his underpants were and did not care. He was above societal courtesies and mandates. He could leap to the heavens and free fall through the galaxies. He was free, dammit, totally free. And one day, they would finally get it.

TIRED

Debbie hated the yoga retreats most of all. She was not fond of meditation and forward bending poses made her dizzy. And he always acted like such a moron. The Neru jacket was bad enough. But his insistence that she call him "Orion" was ridiculous. Period. The whole scene was tired. She wanted to make her escape, to hop the next available plane and get as far away from this impossibly self-important man as she could.

"Squalor is my middle name. We'll get this cleaned up and taken care of in no time." Sloane raised a droopy eye and studied the disturbingly cheerful woman standing in his living room. She had her hands on her hips. "We'll start with these piles of newspaper and then the old plastic grocery bags. My goodness you have so many of them! Of course, there's the matter of the cat poop and the beer cans. And you'll be glad to know I've got just the thing for these awful stains in your carpet." Sloane shifted in his seat and reached for the remote. He wondered how many they'd sent now and how quickly he could make this one go away.

EXACTLY

"That's exactly what I'm talking about," she scolded. Dexter and Cosmo looked up at their mother, then down at the Legos scattered around the living room. Her nostrils flared as she scolded them. They could see up her nose. They hoped she would stop soon. There were spaceships to build and tiny moon battles to attend to.

Celia twirled around the bakery. Every cell in her body tingled. She would try one of everything! The soft croissants beckoned her with their buttery goodness. The éclairs and the little pies mugged cheerfully in the pastry case, as if to say: "Choose us! Choose us!" The maple twists seduced her with their sugary brilliance, and the proud scones, with their assertive blueberry glaze, commanded the display. But it was the mesmerizing cinnamon rolls that most got her attention. They were gooey and big and delightfully sweet; the quintessence of what a pastry should be, now and forever.

PROPAGANDA

Barney stood perplexed in front of the many bins. He started to put his empty coffee cup into one bin but reconsidered. Was it the green one or the blue one? He studied the signs with the little pictures of litter and food. His brain ran around in unwieldy circles. "This is all propaganda," he sighed to himself as he threw his cup on the ground.

Levi liked spicy food and bossy women. His car—a '89 Chevy Impala—was not fast but it was loud. He knew how to two-step and could shoot a mean game of pool. He had real teeth, all of his hair and didn't need pharmaceutical "enhancement" to do his thing. He was living the dream and anyone who disagreed could kiss his ass.

UNDETERRED

She was one paycheck away from disaster, one blink short of beautiful and light years removed from redemption. Still, she was undeterred. She would lean in closer and grind harder. She would look her shitty life square in the eye and fight until she had nothing left.

The universe lifted its gargantuan head and smiled bemusedly. It stared out across the vast cosmos and gave a lengthy stretch. It looked down at all the little beings scurrying about their business, meeting challenges head-on and hoping that this day would bring the miracle. The universe grabbed a handful of stardust and sprinkled it, with love, over the masses below. It so wanted them all to triumph. And today, a few of them would.

SUCCESS

The dog ran down the alley. The steak dangling from his mouth flapped against his little legs with every stride. Gloria screamed as she chased him. She was faster than he'd reckoned on. He dashed underneath a parked car. He could see her feet run circles around the vehicle. He could smell her anger. "Give that back right now," she demanded. He growled and swallowed his spoils in three easy bites. Success.

Her terse expression said it all. There would be no sex tonight. He'd brought home chicken and put on clean pants. He'd even replaced the batteries in the remote without her asking. But still, she was disinterested in his romantic offerings. He took another sip of Mountain Dew and thought hard. Maybe he should have wiped off the counter, or cleaned the litter box. She was such a confusing mystery. If he could only figure out which chore would grant him the keys to the city.

ALLOWING

The last thing he remembered was catching the garter at the reception. And now here he was, thousands of meters under the sea in a submarine full of Danish sailors. Eventually, he'd have to account for himself. But for now, he could not explain what he didn't understand. He looked around at his jolly companions and joined their jaunty cheers. Life is about flow, he figured, about allowing things to happen however they will.

She was a card-carrying narcissist with a mission to kill. She strolled through the room, looking fierce, for sure, in her fine leather jacket and "don't fuck with me" stilettos. She surveyed the scene, sniffing for minions. Her smile was gold. With one nod, she'd have them swimming around her and clamoring for attention. "Such are the dogs," she thought to herself, "begging for bullshit and pleasantries." But she'd suffer these fools only so long. She'd use what she needed and take what she wanted. Her eye was on the prize.

He would don his gay apparel, dammit, and would sing whatever Christmas carols he felt like. He'd drink eggnog and eat fruitcake too. And if he wanted to, he'd wear the blinking antlers. He would defy their cynicism and smug arrogance. He didn't care that they were intellectuals or philanthropists. He wasn't impressed by their advanced pedigree or their bulging bank accounts. His parents were assholes, straight up. Blood may be thicker than water. But Christmas belonged to him.

SURVIVED

Wandeen put out her cigarette and rolled up her sleeves. She wasn't afraid of these two. She'd survived worse, much worse. She bent down and squinted at her charges. Cosmo and Dexter stared back. They'd never seen so many tattoos, or a lady with a moustache like that. They were scared and excited all at the same time. "You smell funny," Dexter blurted out. With that, the mad night was on.

Oscar liked his big monster truck. He liked gunning the engine. He liked gunning the engine in his big monster truck. He liked to park in the lot by the beach. It was exciting when the people strolled by and saw him sitting there in his very big monster truck. It was the best part of life, really. Sitting there like that. Every day, he prayed and thanked Jesus for his good fortune. A truck like that doesn't come along to every man. He was blessed and he knew it.

SWING

"Many can 'bust a groove' as you like to say, but few can swing in the true spirit of the two and the four." She proceeded to demonstrate, shuffling awkwardly across the activity room. Gerald offered his hand to steady her, but she squealed and sashayed away from him. Years ago, his mother sailed off on her own personal happy ship and has been spinning in rapturous revelry ever since. She was frail, delicate and turbocharged. She never remembered his name but was predictably delighted with the candy he always brought. Anymore, that was enough for Gerald.

Her text came hours after the fact. He took a slow sip of coffee and stared at his phone. Her delayed response was an answer in and of itself. He rubbed a hand across his stubble and considered how much patience he had left. Yelling gets the point across. But silence is much meaner. As much as it wrecked him, he needed to put an end to this nonsense. As his mother used to say: "When people tell you who they are, believe them."

GREGARIOUS

Mona was unimpressed with the wine tasting. The gregarious sommelier was tedious and dimwitted. This year's Cabernets were a bore. They lacked depth and clarity. Their bouquets were demure. The finishes were awkward and uninspired. The evening was an affront to her palate. She reached into her bag for the flask. Glenlivet was the only thing that could save her now.

Bob watched his sisters-in-law sitting in a circle, singing in perfect harmony. He hated these family gatherings. He'd rather have a colonoscopy than listen to one more earnest folk song about train whistles, mountaintops and coming home. And the banjos– the god forsaken banjos– made him want to sever his ears off his head. All he wanted was his Wall Street Journal and a glass of scotch, neat. He clapped politely and smiled at his happy wife. She was such a funny little bird. She made him stronger in the craziest of ways.

SHENANIGANS

Karl finished his orange juice, put on his scrubs and made his way to the ER. He wondered what shenanigans they would get into tonight; which body parts he would have to stitch up, what objects he'd have to remove, what lifeless hearts he would have to resurrect. He knew there would be sorrow, urgency, anger and relief. Some would pray. Some would punch a hole in the wall. Some would freeze. Humanity was such a quagmire.

"Imagine floating on a giant cookie in an ice cream sea. The air smells like chocolate and the sun is giant lemon drop, shining just for you. And deep in the night when your bellies are full, you'll rest your head on marshmallow pillows and dream of castles filled with candy and cake." She kissed their foreheads and trembled ever so slightly as she smoothed the blankets over their wiggling bodies. Cosmo and Dexter began their drowsy descent. Grandma was magic. This was something they knew for sure.

ABOUT THE AUTHOR

Katy Bourne is a self-described "basic goober just trying to find her way in the world." By day, she writes promotional copy for musicians and bands. By night, she sings jazz at nightclubs, festivals and special events throughout the Northwest. On her blog, Katy fearlessly digs into a variety of subjects, including the ups and downs of the creative life, parenthood, the music business, Seahawk football and other matters of the heart.

Please visit: www.katy-bourne.com.